Blue in Green

Blue in Green

A NOVELLA BY WESLEY BROWN

BLANK FORMS EDITIONS BROOKLYN, NY

Blue in Green is a work of fiction. The actual events described in the book provide the backdrop to the story, but the actions of the characters, who are based on real people, come from the imagination of the writer. Several biographies and memoirs were read to gain insight into the lives of the individuals portrayed in the book: *Walk Tall: The Music and Life of Julian "Cannonball" Adderley* by Cary Ginell, *Deals with the Devil: And Other Reasons to Riot* by Pearl Cleage, *Coltrane on Coltrane: The John Coltrane Interviews* edited by Chris DeVito, *Miles: The Autobiography* by Miles Davis with Quincy Troupe, *Miles and Me* by Quincy Troupe, *Dark Magus: The Jekyll and Hyde Life of Miles Davis* by Gregory Davis with Les Sussman, *Miles Davis: The Definitive Biography* by Ian Carr, *So What: The Life of Miles Davis* by John Szwed, *Kind of Blue: The Making of the Miles Davis Masterpiece* by Ashley Kahn, *The Blue Moment: Miles Davis's Kind of Blue and the Remaking of Modern Music* by Richard Williams, *Prince of Darkness: A Jazz Fiction Inspired by the Music of Miles Davis* by Walter M. Ellis, *Man Walking on Eggshells* by Herbert Simmons, *Bill Evans: How My Heart Sings* by Peter Pettinger, *Gil Evans: Out of the Cool: His Life and Music* by Stephanie Stein Crease, *To Be, or Not ... to Bop* by Dizzy Gillespie with Al Fraser, *Stormy Weather: The Life of Lena Horne* by James Gavin, *America's Mistress: The Life and Times of Eartha Kitt* by John L. Williams, and *Thelonious Monk: The Life and Times of an American Original* by Robin D. G. Kelley.

I want to express my gratitude to Nell Painter and Glenn Shafer for their generous support in the early stages of working on my book; to my agent Faith Childs who has remained steadfast in her commitment to my work, especially during those fallow periods which every writer experiences, and for her astute engagement with Blank Forms on behalf of the manuscript; to Ciarán Finlayson and Lawrence Kumpf, editors at Blank Forms, who were enormously excited about the book and whose enthusiasm was evident through-out every stage leading to its publication; to my editor Malaika Adero, who was appropriately unsparing in her deep editorial dive into the manuscript, which pulled it out of my comfort zone, helping me to make it more than I thought it could be; to Max Fox whose careful copyediting identified areas of the manuscript where greater clarity was needed; to Beverly Gologorsky, a valued friend whose encouragement of my work over the years has been unwavering; to Charles Lynch: the give and take of our talks are never less than much ado about a great deal of something; to Jamil Blackwell: as long-standing cohorts, we have kept each other up to speed on the sounds of jazz that we continue to listen to in our heads, whether we're talking or not; to Brenda Wilkinson, my first reader, who after reading the book out loud made the point that I should do so myself after each draft in order to hear it more clearly. And finally, many thanks to Julie Brickman, Jennifer Kay, Julia Kirst, Betsy McTiernan, Gay Semel, and Eve Zatt for reading early drafts of the book.

In memory of

Frances Elizabeth Taylor (September 28, 1929–November 17, 2018)
Miles Dewey Davis III (May 26, 1926–September 28, 1991)
Frederick Henry Foss (April 19, 1949–April 23, 2019)
Cheryl Ann Wall (October 29, 1948–April 4, 2020)

The danger is that we have gone so long without asking the question that we have forgotten the answer.

The danger is that we have gone so long taking what we can get that we have forgotten what we wanted.

—Pearl Cleage

AUGUST   25,   1959

"Muthafucka," Miles said under his breath, more in frustration than anger. While smoking a cigarette outside Birdland—after he'd escorted a woman to a cab at the curb—a cop told him to move along.

"I'm working," he said, pointing to the marquee. A smirk curved the cop's mouth.

"Oh, so now they got you showing people in and out the club instead of that midget in a uniform who usually does it."

Like a boxer in the opening round, Miles felt heat rising to his forehead. The words stung for a second.

"You got a problem with what I do inside or what I just got through doing out here?"

"It doesn't matter to me one way or the other. But if it did, I'd do something about it," the cop said.

"If it's about the woman I put in the cab, I guess movies are the only thing you like to see in black and white."

The cop grimaced. He stepped closer, his hands tightening around his nightstick.

"You need to go back inside or get off the street!"

Miles shook his head. He took a drag on his cigarette.

"Did you hear what I said?" The cop angled toward him.

He dropped his cigarette, mashed it under his shoe, and set himself in a boxer's defensive stance. He gave the cop a blinding stare. Suddenly, he heard shoe leather on the pavement behind him. A blow hammered on his head. He went down. Shouts burned his ears. Everything was a blur. All he could do was brace himself for the next crack of pain and protect his mouth.

Blood streamed from a gash across his scalp as he was cuffed and pushed into a squad car. He spotted Cannonball who was now standing in front of the club.

"Call Frances, tell her to come down to the precinct around the corner," he shouted out. "And bring me a change of clothes."

The cops first took him to a nearby hospital. As nurses sutured his wound, he noticed bloodstains on his tailored buttermilk sport coat. This made his foul mood even worse. Then they took him to the precinct, where he was charged with assault and disorderly conduct.

Cannonball and Frances arrived just as the charges were being read. Miles kept himself zipped up tight. Frances saw him and pressed her arms tightly against her stomach. To give her support, Cannonball rested his hand gently on her elbow. Miles saw them and felt his body loosen. A smile creased his mouth, relieved as he was to see his woman and Cannonball. She rushed to him, grabbing a fist of his jacket, and kissed him on the side of the face. Eyeing the cops watching, he broke from the embrace, wanting to take a longer look at these assholes who'd beaten him like a drum, something he would not soon forget.

He made bail and was released. Just before leaving, he shot the cops a cold-blooded stare.

"Let's get the fuck outta here."

"Look at you," Frances said, smiling, once they were on the street.

"You should see the other guys. How many were there anyway?"

"Enough that the outcome was never in doubt." Cannonball said.

"Frances. You bring my clothes?"

"Yes, but why can't you wait until we get home to change?"

"I need to get this blood-stained shit off me. The club ain't closed yet, is it?"

"No," Cannonball said. "They're probably still counting money and cleaning up the place."

"Did y'all do the last set?"

"Folks wanted to stay and the guys wanted to get paid, so they agreed. I told them to go on and play and I'd go to the precinct to see about you."

"I know Trane didn't have no problem with that."

"As a matter of fact, he kept playing his solo while folks went outside to see what all the commotion was about."

"Trane don't hardly say a word except when that horn is in his mouth like a pacifier."

"You should talk. You don't do much of that either. But I think Trane would agree that he's still a babe in the woods, looking for a shed to call his own."

"Well, he's doing it on my dime. So he needs to get busy 'cause I'm about too through with him subletting my band."

Having arrived in front of Birdland, they stood under the canopy.

"I'm gonna split, Miles," Cannonball said.

"Why not. That's what the other cats did."

"What I love about you, Miles, is that you keep yourself and everybody else guessing whether you decided to be hip or it just happened that way."

"Since I'm the darkest berry out here, I'ma keep the rest a y'all in the dark."

Cannonball shook his head. "Frances, I don't know how you put up with him."

There was a lull and she didn't fill it.

"Take care, Frances."

"You too, Cannonball. Thanks for coming with me."

"You should take some time off, Miles. It'd be good for your head."

"My head'll feel better in a couple of days."

"I'm talking about what's inside it," Cannonball said.

The lights in the club were no longer dimmed. Chairs were stacked on tables. Miles saw a few open-collared waiters sitting at tables, guiding food into their mouths more out of habit than hunger, looking like even sitting down after so many hours on their feet didn't give them much comfort.

"Gimme a minute," he said to Frances. "Those dudes look like they're in worse shape than the food they're eating." He wasted no time in the cramped dressing room, changing into the favored gabardine jacket and tapered Italian trousers Frances brought him. He tossed the bloody clothes into a trash basket.

They left the club and crossed to the other side of Broadway where his Ferrari was parked. He looked up at the brightly lit letters spelling ALVIN HOTEL, the place Lester Young, otherwise known as President or Prez, lived before he left town permanently, so to speak.

"What're you thinking about?" she asked.

"Nothing important," he said, kissing her on the mouth.

He was thinking about Prez. How'd he become a ghost before he gave it up altogether. He recalled with affection that it was Lester Young who assigned him the nickname Midget. A few years before, they'd recorded together in Europe. At every performance, he was wowed by Prez's cradle-will-rock hold on his saxophone, the sound coming through sideways, blowing a lightly toasted buzz out of his throat. Not lost on him was the notion that despite Prez's dizzying lingo and slippery avoidance of a world cruising for a bruising, it still found him.

They were silent on the drive home. She touched his thigh.

"How're you doing?"

He turned his face toward her.

"Are you just putting up with me?"

"That was Cannonball talking, not me. He was just messing with you."

"Yeah, like when he put his hand on your arm."

"He was just being supportive."

"Why didn't you say something about what he said?"

"Because what he said has nothing to do with how I feel."

They pulled up in front of the apartment building. He sat back and kept his door closed.

"You go ahead in."

"You're not coming?"

"I'ma drive around awhile."

"Why do you want to drive around?"

"You trying to keep tabs on me?"

"It was a question, Miles."

"No, it ain't!"

"I only meant, after what happened tonight, I was feeling the need for us to be together."

"Don't tell me what I need."

"I don't have to. Isn't that why we're together?"

"Get the fuck out the car."

She winced, then got out of the car and started to slam the door but thought better of it. The tires grabbed rubber as he sped off.

*   *   *

He thought about Prez and Lady Day. Prez had died the March before, while Miles was recording his latest album, and she'd passed in July, just a month before his current gig at Birdland. Miles saw Billie the year before at the Persian Room in the Plaza Hotel. He drove to the hotel near 59th Street and Fifth Avenue, looking up at the skyscraper topped off with what reminded him of church steeples. Yeah, a cathedral for the fuckin' rich. Columbia Records held a party to celebrate the success of the jazz division. It was a

Who's Who of jazz royalty, including his sextet, Lady Day, and the Duke. Before the various bands played, there was a reception. He sat at a table with Billie. He was thrilled to be there. They'd bumped into each other over the years, but never actually spent that much time together. He always thought Billie was beautiful, especially her thickly fleshed mouth. But he could tell the rumors were true. Her face was drained of its former fullness and her swollen hands were in gloves up to her elbows. But she showed no signs of caving: her hair pulled back in a bun, chandelier earrings, the signature gardenia pinned to her hair, a drop-dead lavender pants suit. She knew how to dress.

"Well, here we are at last," Billie said. "What took us so long?"

"I guess, bad luck and trouble," he said, unable to keep his shyness under wraps.

"Miles," she asked, "How'd your voice get so low?"

"I had these polyps removed and I wasn't supposed to talk for a few weeks. But something happened at a rehearsal that got on my nerves and I cursed. It wouldn't've been so bad except it was the one nerve I was saving up for some more important shit!"

"Ethel Waters once said I sang like my shoes were too tight. But it wasn't my shoes. It was my life. I had this hollow log way down in me that my voice had to come out of. And that's how the Blues was born."

"...And how we got into the business known as 'show,'" he said.

"Speaking of the 'show' in business, I've heard about you turning away from the audience when you ain't playing. Now that you up close, I get it. You a pretty muthafucka. I see why women and men got their noses wide open, begging for more. But with your back turned, you telling 'em—your eyes may water, your teeth may grit, but none of the rest a me is you gonna get."

"I just want them to listen to the music."

"That's all well and good. But the word I got was that when you play a ballad, women open their legs and you turn away so you won't be distracted."

"That's bullshit."

"I'm not sayin it's true, but it could be. But if I were you, I wouldn't get too strung out on that. Expecting a lotta folks to hear what you putting out there is a waste a time. Too many come to eat you alive. That's why you gotta make sure to listen to your damn self, 'cause no matter what, the show'll go on with or without you."

"I wonder who came up with the 'show must go on?'" he asked.

"Probably a club owner. They some foul-weather muthafuckas!"

"You know Billie, you definitely got me beat when it comes to making muthafucka sound like sweet thunder."

"Don't worry, you'll catch up. I'm just about mutha-fucked out."

"No way, Billie. You still got a long way to ride."

"Tell that to the feds!"

Miles saw the dark quarter-moon brows lift her eyes into a stare at something far away. He decided not to say any more. Billie snapped out of it as soon as she heard the announcement for the first set to begin. She wasn't lying about coming to her last go-round. The final indignity was being handcuffed to a hospital bed. But that afternoon, he got more than an earful as Billie fought the good fight. She shimmied her shoulders, moved her hands back and forth like she was flirting with the good life, cocking her head, listening to the pianist, Mal Waldron, do a finger roll over the keys as a possible direction she might want to take. She pressed her lips together to indicate "hmm, that might work," opening her mouth slightly, as though hearing the words before she could see them with her eyes, smell them through her nose, and taste them on her tongue, coming out like she was thoroughly fed up: *There ain't nothing I ever do / Or nothing I ever say, / that folks don't criticize me.* Taking her mouth out of neutral, she twisted it to a corner with an attitude that didn't give a shit: *But I'm gonna do just as I want to anyway / And don't care if they all despise me.*

Before delivering another mouthful of sass, Miles shook his head as if to say, "You got it, Billie, the rest of us still trying to find it."

She finally launched the song with *If I took a notion to jump right in the ocean / Ain't nobody's business if I do.*

He heard the raspy edge of life scratching in her throat, chasing the Blues away, threatening, "kiss my unruly ass . . ."

Miles was still in a deep funk from getting his ass whipped to a fare-thee-well. He'd decided his business was nobody's business except the police. He remembered his set after Billie's. He'd wanted to bring the temperature down a notch. So, he chose "If I Were a Bell" as the opener.

He snapped out the tempo, muting the fire in his trumpet, but not its burn. He didn't have the lightning-streak speed or large brassy sound of Roy Eldridge or Dizzy Gillespie, piercing the heights of the nosebleed section of the crow's nest in movie theaters, where Negroes had to sit. But like Lady Day, he found his calling in fewer notes, fresh-squeezed through his horn without any trace of pulp.

He was pleased with the set. The rhythm section, Bill Evans, Paul Chambers, and Jimmy Cobb, held up their end, with Jimmy's drumsticks shivering on his ride cymbal on top and Paul's deep bass groans at the bottom. Bill struck his usual pose during a solo, his head nearly touching the ivories. He picked the pockets of Monk, but returned what he'd taken with interest, hearing "If I Were a Bell" in his fingers, a running brook of clear water ringing in the keys, *If I were a season / I'd surely be spring*. Miles played a rubber-band stretch away from the melody, shaping his sound to mouth the lyrics, *If I were a lamp I'd light / Or if I were a banner I'd wave*. Ben Webster often said how important knowing the words were on a ballad, so they sang through your horn. At a point in his solo, the words were voiced through his trumpet: *All I can say / Is if I were a bridge / I'd be burning*. He felt Lady Day's bridge burning, and finding relief getting to the bridge of this bell-ringing, ding-dong tune. He faded out with a trill, remembered from child-hood, using his tongue to spit out the shells of pumpkin seeds . . . Cannonball began taking his turn and complemented his quick mouth with words, having big fun showing off his chops on alto, speeding up the tempo, high and low, slowing down enough to give props to the tune with *All I can say / If I were a gate / I'd be swinging*.

Miles once asked Trane why he played so long. Trane had said, "It took that long to get it all out." It was no different at the Persian Room the year before. Trane leaped in, turning what had been done to "If I Were a Bell" inside out before he took his turn. Miles felt that Trane played backwards, like from the get-go of a tune, already knowing how he heard it so many times before, but wanting to find out how he might hear it if he tried to follow what was hidden in what he didn't know. That might lead him back to the beginning, maybe revealed in *Ask me how do I feel / From this chemistry lesson I'm learning*, to a place where he had begun. At least that's what Miles imagined.

*   *   *

After Miles screeched away in his Ferrari, Frances steadied her hand before she put the key in the door and stepped into the apart-ment. She took a breath, went into the bedroom, slipped off her shoes and lay on the bed. She remembered her father's response when Miles asked for his blessing when he proposed marriage. He had refused.

19

"Frances doesn't need my consent to marry, if that's what she truly wants to do. But I will say, you both need to be saved from yourselves. You'll probably turn out worse if you marry." The whole business of him approaching her father made her heart flutter, but she really had no prior desire to marry. And her first love, ballet, was waiting for Frances, just about to raise the curtain. If she had any apprehension about pursuing dance, seeing the movie, *The Red Shoes* with Moira Shearer had removed any doubt. In the story, a ballerina is torn between two loves: a man and her career. The fear of losing him drives her to leap to her death from a balcony. But a question was left unanswered. Had she taken her own life or were the red shoes the culprit, knowing better than the ballerina that they could not live without each other? Frances was convinced she would never betray her slippers or do anything to jeopardize the life they shared

*   *   *

Not knowing what to do with herself, Frances thought about Miles saying he didn't want to be told what he needed. She went to the closet, took out her old ballet slippers and tights, undressed, and put them on. Looking at herself in a mirror, she remembered how, early on, teachers always spoke glowingly of her legs. She inherited them from her mother and didn't have to be told of their beauty. What interested her far more was experiencing a growing curiosity and adventurousness in herself as she emerged from adolescence. She knew she wasn't as beautiful as, say, Dorothy Dandridge, who was looked upon in awe without actually being seen. Frances believed herself willing to comfortably close the space keeping her at a distance from others. Growing up in Chicago, she never questioned choosing to live her life in this way.

In 1947, Frances auditioned for the Katherine Dunham Dance Company. Her father was there—and always by her side as she pursued her dream. She loved his name, Maceo, which meant "gift of God." They watched a rehearsal, marveling at the astonishing dancers. When Dunham demonstrated a particular move, she sprung spider-like from the web of the floor.

"This is something you really want to do," he said to Frances, not out of any doubt about her decision, but only to see the desire in her face. Dunham was a formidable figure. She commanded attention. Frances went through a sequence of moves she was asked to execute. Breathing heavily, she came away convinced that everything she did was a complete disaster. Dunham gave no sign to what she thought one way or the other. After what seemed to Frances like an hour, she stretched the corners of her mouth, raising her cheeks into stones. A glint in her eyes followed a nod of her head.

After joining the Company, Frances toured Europe and South America. In 1948 she was invited to perform with another company, the Paris Opera Ballet. She was the first Negro to achieve this distinction. She was a sensation. People called her the "Leslie Caron of the Tropics." Now, here she was, a decade later, standing in front of a mirror in ballet slippers that had been idle for years. She inhaled and assumed the five basic ballet positions, believing they were alive in her torso, arms, legs, feet, and toes. She named them out loud: "First position: toes apart, heels squeezed together, feet firm, arms in the shape of a beach ball in front of belly, chest open, shoulders down, back engaged. Second position: feet and legs out to the side, hip-distance apart, arms rounded out to the side. Third position: feet turned outward, heels touching arch, one in front of the other, one arm in front of the body, the other to the side. Fourth position: feet separated, one in front of the other, then parallel, heel of one foot to toe of the other, squared, one arm rounded out to the side, the other raised above the head, slight bend to the elbows and wrists. Fifth position: feet turned outward, distance of one foot placed in front of the other, first big toe extends past each heel, arms raised above the head, slightly forward, elbows and wrists slightly bent."

She repeated each position several times without stopping. Feeling sweat on her face, under her arms, and between her legs, it felt right. Wasn't this how to approach life: centered, balanced, activated, and fully prepared to meet it head on?

This was one of the many lessons Dunham taught her that she had never learned before in class. Early in Frances's tenure with the Company, Dunham asked her to stay after a rehearsal. Frances feared that this would be the moment she was told that her dancing had not met the troupe's high standards.

"How long did you study ballet?" Dunham asked.

"Since I was eight," she said emphatically, not wanting to reveal how intimidated she still was in Dunham's presence.

"What was that like?"

"I loved it!"

"Why?"

"Ballet grounded me. It taught me that the floor was both a friend and a foe. I'd plant my feet and push down, using enough leg strength to lift me up into flight above the floor. Since the floor didn't move, it either broke my fall or me. I didn't break. And I learned to speak and be heard."

"By whom?"

"Myself."

"Just yourself?"

"No. But that's where I had to start."

"Do you think what you had to say is still worth hearing?"

"Yes."

"What makes you think so?"

"Because I've always felt that way."

"Why didn't you continue with ballet?"

"I've never stopped. I carry it with me."

"You know, there are some ballet masters who believe that dance teaches the dancer how to play their body like an instrument—like a piano."

"If they believe that, I want to be that—an instrument."

"How do you plan to do that?"

"Well, that's why I'm here. To learn how."

"What did you think of the rules of ballet?"

"I absorbed them for ten years!"

"That's not what I asked."

"They were rigorous, demanding, and necessary."

Dunham's mouth surrendered to a hint of a smile. "Your ballet training has served you well. It's given you power and impressive execution. And you've got attitude that's not defensive. It just is."

"Thank you," Frances said. Some praise at last.

"Don't thank me too soon. Any thanks is all yours. But there is something else."

"What is that?"

"When I was a child," Dunham said, "I would tell my elders of actual events I remembered from my birth and before. They were astounded. I can also anticipate the future. In terms of my Company, I know how my dancers will execute specific movements from my choreography before they perform them. You are a rare exception. The other was Eartha Kitt. Do you know her?"

"I know who she is. But I've never met her."

"You will. She's as gifted as you are, but with a difference."

"In what way?"

"When she was angry, it turned up in her performance and not in a good way. But that anger was part of what made her exceptional. Of course, whenever I tried to anticipate her movements away from dance, I was way out of my depth. With you, there's something else I haven't been able to anticipate."

"What's that?"

"Your anger. Where is it?"

"I get upset like anyone else."

"That's not the same thing."

"It's something I've always tried to control."

"Why?"

"I was taught not to let it get in my way."

"That's my point. I want to see it get in your way! And how you express it, while still remaining under control."

"I don't know if I can do that the way you want."

"It's not about the way I want. It's the way you have to want it— if as you say, you want to speak and be heard. Why don't I feel you giving yourself over to the drums in your performance?" She pulled over a conga drum. "You haven't allowed your body to feel its way inside the hollow space that makes the sound, answering the call from the drummer's hands, talking through the skin of the drum. Give me your wrist." Frances extended it and Dunham placed two fingers near the bone.

"Do you feel it?" she asked.

"Yes."

"Your pulse is no different from feeling the beat coming from below the skin of a drum. If you can feel it, you can find it. And if you can find it, you can hear it."

Frances was upset by Dunham's belief that channeling her unacknowledged anger would strengthen her performance. But she was right. Since Dunham never mentioned it again, there was no way of knowing if anger was the reason for feeling her body loosening to the enticing drums, turning her spine to bamboo, hearing her grunts, arching her back in undulating waves, freeing her shoulders to tremble, and letting her arms give way to ropes.

*   *   *

In Miles's absence, Frances was left to confront a rush of memories, some wonderful and others not. Returning to New York after years touring with Dunham, she married briefly. She gave birth to a son.

23

She was not prepared to see Miles coming in the opposite direction walking up Broadway one afternoon. Impeccably dressed, as always, his simmering eyes and glowing, pitch-dark skin weakened her. Within an arm's length, he gently took hold of her wrists: "Now that I've found you, I'm not going to let you go."

After some time together, she shared what for her was an amusing anecdote about taking Paris by storm, performing with the Paris Opera Ballet.

He lashed out at her. "Fuck that! I'd never let myself be called the Marlon Brando of jazz!"

"I know being called the 'Leslie Caron of the Tropics' was supposed to be a compliment, but it had very little to do with me. Even though I was singled out, ballet companies were not looking for someone like me, except as a temporary novelty."

"That's what I'm saying. The only way to compare you to anybody would be to call you the Frances Taylor of dance."

Oh, I do love this man, she thought. She was thrilled beyond words. It didn't matter if he was angry. To hear him say that told her he believed she was a person unto herself. When he proposed the second time, she accepted, hoping he still believed her to be the Frances Taylor of dance. But it was as important for her to know what her father and mother believed.

*   *   *

Whenever she was in her father's presence, the glimmer in his eyes told Frances that he believed she always demanded the best of herself. She wondered what he would think of her decision to marry Miles.

"Are you surprised, Daddy?" she asked, unable to detect anything of what he felt about her news.

"You always surprise me, Frances."

"Do I?"

"That's why you're such a joy to me."

"And now?"

"You marrying Miles doesn't change that feeling."

"But you didn't think I should've married him before."

"He wanted to get married. You never said you did."

"Are you going to wish me luck, Daddy?"

A frown played on his mouth. "Why would I do that?"

"Why wouldn't you?"

"Because to have luck, you have to be ready for it—which you've always been."

"Do you think I'm ready for this?"

"You weren't the first time. Maybe this time, it'll be different."

"What do you think of him?"

"He is a truly gifted musician. And he's driven—just like you."

"That's a good thing, isn't it?" she asked with some urgency.

"For whom?"

"For both of us. To have something we both love that's not only each other."

He fixed his eyes on her. "Is that what you want?"

"Yes, Daddy."

"Then I hope you're as ready to be lucky in your love of him."

Frances's mother always kept herself quiet, as though holding her breath, until releasing what she had to say with calm determination.

"Mother. Miles asked me to marry him again."

"He is persistent."

"He is."

"What about you?"

"I've taken a little longer to make up my mind."

"What changed it?"

"I did."

"Why?"

"Before I didn't have room in my life."

"You believe there's enough room for both of you now?"

"Yes."

"And your son?"

"I know you and Daddy were there for me when Jean Pierre was born. And I want him with us . . ."

"Don't worry. Whenever you're ready."

"It was a mistake with his father."

"Yes, it was."

"I thought we would make it."

"I know."

"Did you think we would?"

"I hoped for the best."

"Is that how you felt with Daddy?"

"With us it was more than hope."

"What was it?"

"We just knew."

"What did you know?"

"That we could live together without ever hurting each other more than either of us could bear."

"I wish I'd known that."

"That depended on knowing the kind of man he was."

"What kind of man do you think he was?"

"I'm more interested in the kind of woman you are, which I haven't always understood."

"What didn't you understand?"

"Your will to do what you set your mind to. Your father knew this a lot sooner that I did. That's why he encouraged you and took you to all your classes and out of town recitals."

"Mother, you were very supportive."

"Somewhat reluctantly. You were becoming a daughter I didn't recognize. Someone I could no longer see in myself. I resented you. And I resented your father seeing in you something he didn't see in me. But I didn't see it in me either."

"Mother. Are you proud of me?"

"More than you know."

It did her heart good, coming from the mother she knew, just to hear those few words and not think about her given name: Cozy. They embraced, their bodies barely touching.

*   *   *

The adulation Frances received for her performances in off-Broadway revivals of *Porgy and Bess* and *Carmen*, and the offer of a role in the Broadway production of *West Side Story* compared favorably to the accolades she received touring with the Dunham Company. All eyes were on her, on stage or off. She drew people to what she discovered in herself, showing no interest in their attention. Instead, it was her attention which everyone else wanted, including Miles. He loved her olive skin and eyes that could thrill, blowing into the mute of his trumpet, like a puff through a dandelion ball, whispering across the floor of his breath in what he called "Fran-Dance." Hearing him play "Fran-Dance" for the first time, she felt lifted with the ease of breathing, allowing herself to imagine giving bodily shape to every tremor, shriek, growl, trill, hum, and cry of his playing.

Landing the role in *West Side Story*, Frances believed he would be proud. During rehearsals, he would call the theater frequently

26

to check on her. If they went out to a restaurant, he became irate if a man looked in her direction. One evening soon after the opening, she was surprised to see him waiting in his Ferrari outside the theater. She got in, leaned over to kiss him, but he turned away.

"What's the matter?"

"This isn't going to work."

"What isn't going to work?"

"You have to leave the show."

"Why?"

"Because you need to be at home."

"I don't understand."

"What's there to understand? I just told you what I want you to do."

"Why would I give up something I love?"

"Because you're my woman and you need to be with me."

"I am with you."

"But you're not where I want you to be—which is at home when I get there."

She wanted to scream, but swallowed it. "What about composing 'Fran-Dance?'" she asked.

"I wrote that for you."

"But you want to take away the 'dance' part of what you wrote—that's the other half of who I am."

"I'm taking it away from all those folks who see you perform."

"But Miles, I dance for them and myself."

"When you dance, you give all of yourself and there's nothing left."

"There's always something left."

"Not enough for me," he said, pressing against the car door.

"I never feel there's not enough for me when you play."

"That's 'cause not as many people come to hear me in clubs."

"Is this what you meant when you said you'll never let me go?"

"I'm done talking about it!"

*   *   *

The danger signs were evident before *West Side Story*. After the off-Broadway revival of *Porgy and Bess*, Miles became interested in recording an album of portions of the score from the Gershwin opera. Gil Evans did the arrangements and conducted a full orchestra, including members of Miles's sextet. He never allowed her to

27

attend recording sessions and rarely talked about his music. But a guy known to musicians as Freddie Freeloader, a grungy, scraggly bearded Black man seen by Frances at clubs where Miles played, was a part-time bartender, sometime bodyguard who ran errands, often showing up in a sun visor, wearing a string of trumpet mouthpieces around his neck and two drumsticks strapped, Western style, to his waist. He talked in a salty jazz argot, seeing himself as a kind of roving disc jockey and jackleg emcee. He was sometimes allowed to be a proverbial fly on the wall at recording sessions.

Frances heard rumors of him holding court around musicians, regaling them with stories of jam sessions and club dates he attended or imagined:

From the get-go, there's a full-blast orchestral screech of reeds and brass, and the presence of "The Buzzard Song" arrives as an ominous sign when Porgy spots a bird of prey at the same moment as the menacing Sportin' Life appears in Catfish Row. An eye-opening roar, deep in the belly of a tuba gives way to Miles playing an ear-piercing wail, full of fear and worry about the Catfish Row living within himself and his unmuted wolf howl, as the buzzard's warning of the worst in all of us. There's no feeling of peril, even as Miles plays "Bess, You Is My Woman Now" shifting his tone away from "telling" her she is his woman. Standing in for Porgy, he muffles each note, shyly, covering his mouth, scraping the sole of his shoe against the sidewalk, trying not to tell Bess whose woman she is, as an undisputed truth. She can't help but smile, hearing the orchestra chiming in with what sounds like: "We got to hear where this is going"— but anyone who knows Miles would say that when his rock-hard leather-tough face splits into a shit-eating grin, a woman's got his nose open Mack truck–wide. So he cozies up to his heart enough to say with a hope and a prayer, "Bess, is you my woman, now?" trembling out the bell of his horn ... Now, if you'd indulge me bending your ear a bit longer, there's a part of Porgy and Bess *that ain't from the opera. It's something Gil Evans thought up called "Gone," beginning with a fierce battle between Miles and the drummer, Philly Joe Jones, egged on by the brass section which Miles saw as reminiscent of the 1957 middleweight championship bout between Sugar Ray Robinson, a kid from Detroit who danced in the street for pennies, and Gene Fullmer, a brawler, not a skilled boxer, only capable of throwing haymakers ... The brass leaps in quickly, cheering for what is to come, followed by Philly Joe's paradiddle punches. Miles blows into the fray, snapping off crackling chin music, answering the opening snare jabs thrown by Philly Joe: bah-bah-bum-bum-bum-bahh-dum, and horning in on Philly Joe's rim shots. Miles settles in, quiets his tone, avoiding the bass drum slug fest Philly Joe wants. Next you hear the spitting sounds of Miles's foot speed, circling around Philly Joe's drum kit, sizing him up, looking for an opening to get inside the quick stick attack on his snare. But Philly Joe loads up on Miles with heavy bass pedal tom-tom-booms with a crash of high hat and cymbals, while the cat, personifying the "Birth of the Cool," plays possum before instinct in his hips, shoulder, and elbow unleash a left hook vibrato, putting Fullmer down and out. After the recording, Miles called Sugar Ray's one-punch K.O. "as perfect a note I have yet to play." He definitely takes to heart the Sugar Man's boxing philosophy: "You don't think. It's all instinct. If you stop to think, you're 'gone'..." I'm outta here, y'all. Catch you at the next gig.*

*   *   *

Frances had no way of knowing how prophetic Freddie Freeloader's telling of Miles's admiration for Sugar Ray Robinson's knockout of Gene Fullmer was until she made a casual remark to Miles about running into a male friend of hers on the street. He reacted on instinct and she was "gone," looking up at him from the floor. No one had ever struck her before. He apologized profusely but she said nothing as she struggled to get up.

"Miles. Do you hit the women who call you on the phone?"

His eyes were lit matches. Instinctively, she raised her arm and watched his eyes begin to water. He squeezed them shut, took a deep breath, pursed his lips and blew, as though about to play. He left the room with her still on the floor.

Later, in the apartment, he told her about his chronic hip pain and how he was taking painkillers. What he didn't tell her, she already knew. He was using cocaine and no longer living his life at its own speed.

*   *   *

A photograph of her and Miles was put on the cover of *Porgy and Bess,* a shot of the two of them, seated, their faces hidden and little shown of the rest of their bodies. Miles composed the shot. He kept a firm grip on his trumpet, and her two fingers dangled near the valves. Her dress revealed a knee and part of her thigh. This was a first for Frances, to be involved in any aspect of his recordings. And she loved the result—at the time. After he hit her, she saw it differently. His grip around the valves looked like a fist, pulling the trumpet tightly against his stomach. She now noticed how her fingers barely touched the trumpet, showing tentativeness about getting any closer to something so much a part of him. Her presence in the photograph was all about him. She was a prop, an eye-catching teaser. The message was: you are my woman.

*   *   *

Miles's philosophy was summed up in his long-held belief that he roll with whatever bullshit came at him. Cops had shaken his belief. He had taken his cues from Prez and Lady Day, but if they rolled with anything, it was into an early grave. He wondered why he was so stressed by those lyrics from "If I Were a Bell": *Ask me how I feel / Little me with my quiet upbringing...*

He was a scrawny little muthafucka, but his upbringing was in no way quiet. His parents, Miles Dewey Davis II and Cleota H. Henry, were upper-crust middle class Negroes who taught him, his older sister Dorothy, and younger brother Vernon that they were special and expected to excel. Their philosophy: present yourself like every day is a celebration of yourself. His mother wore furs and designer hats; his father wore suits and waist coats. The children dressed accordingly. He was the kid decked out in knickers and a double-breasted jacket down to his knees. Looking back, he could only laugh his head off, thinking he was being groomed to look like a little old man at the tender age of nine. Much later, he realized what his mother was trying to teach him: clothes don't make the man. It's the other way around. For too many people, the quality of what they wear doesn't matter, since they are no more than hangers for the clothes on their backs. It was how you wear them. It frightened him when his mother wore a fox-head stole. There weren't many women who could pull off a dead fox draped around their neck.

Miles had a tendency toward shyness and keeping his head down. His mother broke him of the habit, making a fist and knocking him under his chin. He learned to look people in the eye no matter who they were, and adopted his mother's unwavering stare that no one would be foolish enough to meet at risk of retinal burns...

The voices of Miles's parents were ever in his ears, since he was still reeling from being blindsided by those fuckin' cops and unable to do anything about it. He needed the comfort of their proud, domineering presence.

CLEOTA: *Being better than other people is not the same as being superior. And you need to figure that out for yourself. Bourgeois Negroes think they're better than anyone else, especially white folks. They don't understand they're still comparing themselves to the same people they're looking down on. You never want to be somebody else because you're dark skinned or for any other reason. That's a waste of time. Learn how to "get ugly" with people who think you're ugly. Let them know that you being dark will be the least of their worries if they mess with you. Don't listen to these trifling niggers, spending all their time talking about what they have going for themselves because of what they call the "family jewels" between their legs. You're much better off using your time to cultivate the diamond district in your head.*

MILES DEWEY II: *You're going to have to deal with people who'll resent you for having what they don't have. They'll underestimate you, assuming your heart pumps soda pop. You need to prove to those muthafuckas you got Jack Daniels running in your veins. If that's too rich for their blood, get down to their level and tell 'em you got rotgut in your fists, if that's more to their liking. What I've learned from dentistry is that you can play games for a little while, but you need your mouth and teeth all your life. You look into people's mouths long enough, and you see, not only are their teeth as sad as their sorry-ass lives, but given the two places where the good Lord split them, all the shit they talk is redundant.*

Miles had difficulty regarding a lot coming out of his parents' mouths as prayer book material. His mother could talk all she wanted about ugly. But she wasn't above putting the ugly stick on him from hand to mouth, not necessarily in that order. As a child, he was called Buckwheat. But along the way, he made it work for him. He looked up the word and discovered eating buckwheat could cause serious skin rash, itching, swelling, and difficulty breathing. He decided to aspire to become a serious side effect to other people's malicious put downs. Despite his father's advice to kick ass and take names, it was unlikely he'd kick much ass, let alone take any names. But he came around to his mother's point of view.

31

If he was taken lightly, as no more than an ink spot on the white paper of this fuckin' country, he'd make 'em regret it.

*   *   *

For the longest, Miles could not quite get his head around why his parents were so driven by anger. Usually, the first word out of his father's mouth when he got up was "Fuck!" Later on, he decided the reason had to do with having to live another day under the same roof with the mother of his children. These sentiments were shared by his mother concerning life with his father. Making each other miserable had been the thing which kept them together. They needed each other like the ax needs the tree. Neither wanted to be the tree, and neither accepted being the tree. If their arguments were interrupted by some pressing business, they picked them up again afterward, like dueling musicians playing together. His mother was a trained violinist and wanted him to study the instrument. He was not interested. Just the way it was held, leaning your cheek and chin against it, reminded him of taking a nap. And the use of the bow to play seemed as though the sound was far removed from him. The trumpet was in your face. You hold it in your hand, almost in a fist, using the fingers of the other hand to change the tone. Blowing through the mouthpiece made you feel you were in control of the sound. He also had the example of musicians his father knew in St. Louis, across the river from their home in East St. Louis, Illinois. Many of them, trumpet players, were smart dressers with an impressive swagger.

Overruling Miles's mother, his father bought him his first trumpet. He studied with commitment and dedication. At age fourteen, he met Clark Terry, a local trumpet player. Seeing some promise in the youngster, Terry asked Miles's parents if he could take him to jam sessions. This was the beginning of his apprenticeship. He came away from these trials by fire burned but not bowed. The culminating event was when he heard the Billy Eckstine Band booked at the Plantation Club in East St. Louis. The band had a jaw-dropping roster including Dizzy Gillespie, Charlie Parker, Art Blakey, and Sarah Vaughan. An act of providence, a trumpet player stricken by an ailment, provided him the opportunity to fill in. "B," as Billy was called by members in the band, never let up on Miles, treating him as his flunky. It was a test for all young upstarts who assumed they would be treated with respect when they'd done nothing to deserve it. Miles took the insults in stride, believing he wasn't half bad. But he was not nearly good enough to be asked to join the band.

Graduating from high school couldn't have come soon enough. He collected his sheepskin and was on the first train smoking to 52nd Street in New York City. He soon experienced a series of life-altering moments. He took imaginative flights of musical delirium. Scuffled to keep up. Found himself lost in the skids but climbed his way out. He played "'Round Midnight" at the 1955 Newport Jazz Festival. And after all that, got his head bashed in just when he was discarding what he had been and was on the verge of discovering, with the departure of Cannonball, Trane, and Bill, a change of direction yet to be determined.

*   *   *

Frances, still in her tights and ballet slippers, stared at Miles's trumpet case. She asked herself, was it the man or the brilliant musician who initially attracted her? She loved his deep purple skin, giving a reflected luster to anyone coming anywhere near him. There were those long fingers she loved to watch pressing down on the valves of his trumpet, producing not-to-be-forgotten, heart-quaking sounds, the fingers reminding her of narrow strips of dark licorice, sending shivers through her wherever he put them.

They grew closer but Miles was unpredictable, picking fights and flying into rages over things Frances believed to be inconsequential.

"How is it you never learned to cook before we got together," he asked, during a meal he prepared for the two of them.

"My parents didn't insist on it. They made sacrifices so I could focus on ballet."

"And how far did that get you?"

"Whatever the reasons why I didn't continue in ballet, I knew I was good enough. That's all that mattered to me."

"Didn't your parents ever talk to you about being Black?"

"They never talked about color."

"Nobody ever called you a nigger?"

"They did. But I knew who I was and never let it bother me."

"You really believe that shit."

"You forget, my parents were Christian Scientists. They instilled in me a belief that the Father, Son, and Holy Ghost were all I needed to give me the inner strength to overcome any challenge, mental or physical. Any setback was just a test."

"Just a test! You don't know from nothing about a test. I was tested by the toughest muthafuckas there ever was. When I first hit the scene, the cats laughed me off the bandstand. Once I got my shit together, it wasn't over. I had to put up with the clubs. The dressing rooms the size of a closet. The tuxedoed and evening-gowned rich and famous, slumming and shining me on about how great I am. Others dressed like they're going to the beach. The last thing they're interested in is the music, except for a few like my man Freddie, who are all ears. Having to contend with waiters taking orders, clinking glasses, and drunks. A fucked-up scene all around."

Frances gave what Miles said some thought. What, on the surface, appeared to be the manageable aggravations from unruly patrons, she felt was something far more dispiriting, prowling around on two legs. Given his extraordinary gifts as an artist, reacting to anything within earshot required his total focus on the band, tuning out everything else. This was completely at odds with her experience performing. She felt the presence of the audience, but never their voices, which would have been total disrespect. Those coming backstage afterward were, for the most part, dancers and choreographers, among whom she had spent most of her life. Their exquisitely sculpted bodies reflected her view of the world, one that was self-contained and beautifully orchestrated. Unlike concert halls, for dancers, the club environment was so disabling to their creative impulses that performing under such conditions was an act of heroism. She respected that. Miles was one of those who prevailed and that made her love him even more, despite being at the mercy of his demons.

*   *   *

First thing when he arrived in New York, Miles was on a mission to find Bird. But it was Bird who found him. And when he finally got the opportunity to play with him, Miles learned that it wasn't any easier to find him musically than personally. He was always somewhere else. The actual meeting occurred as Miles was smoking a cigarette during a break at Minton's in Harlem. Nothing really dramatic happened, just Bird coming up behind him, saying he'd heard Miles was looking for him. Ballooning with excitement, Miles let loose a torrent of words, not altogether clear what he was saying. A mischievous smile spread into Bird's mouth, seeing Miles was out of breath.

"What else did you want to tell me?" he asked.

"I'll think of something," Miles said.

Bird laughed and embraced him. For the rest of the night, he began to get some inkling of Bird's personality. He exuded enormous curiosity checking Miles out, leaving him a bit unnerved.

Having finally found him, Miles was determined to get himself to wherever he played. Bird breathed like anyone else, but when he inhaled and exhaled through his saxophone, ideas were harvested. There was no one like him. He made distinctions between remembering and memories. There were many things Bird didn't remember, like gigs and rehearsals. It seemed to Miles that musicians, himself included, did remember a great many things, but found it difficult to summon up memories—at least not with the clarity of Bird. He shared with Miles how he replicated the rapid-fire delivery of Kansas auctioneers, who took multiple bids simultaneously and spit words at livestock auctions.

His solos were a stampede of notes at a clip no one could follow or react to, changing tempos at intervals of seconds, leaving Miles's efforts gagging on a trail of notes. Bird split to another tune before they knew it. On this night, they were at a jam session at the Three Deuces at 52nd Street. Miles attempted some lame-ass face-saving remark: "At least I knew the tunes being played." Bird and Dizzy only laughed at his use of "know" in the past tense, when he couldn't even keep up with what was going on in the present.

Miles was undeterred, spending just about every waking moment up in Bird and Dizzy's faces, bugging them to pull his coat, getting him within striking distance of what he needed to learn. Bird's approach was cagey. He said very little, sending Miles on a number of errands, musically, to see if he sank or began to swim. On one occasion, playing at Minton's, Bird walked off the bandstand in the middle of the chorus and left the club. Miles was horrified that he'd been left hanging. Somehow, with the help of the rhythm section, he got through the rest of the tune without completely embarrassing himself. Bird returned about a half hour later.

"Why'd you leave like that," Miles said, really pissed.

"I needed to do something."

Miles wondered if Bird split to make a score. It was well known that he had a serious jones.

"I was up there all by myself."

Bird gave him a bright-eyed smile. "That's the good news."

"What do you mean?"

"You kept playing and had to find your own way. Following me would've only added to the bad news, having to listen to you trying to play catch up."

"But it was embarrassing."

"Not as embarrassing as you were before I left."

"I appreciate your point, Bird, but not how you made it."

"Don't worry, little brother, you'll get over it. And if you don't, you'll get over that too."

That's the kind of shit Bird pulled! You never knew what he would do next. Just as he played, he was a man of tight lips and even more mischief. He had no interest in telling Miles what to do, but preferred putting him through endless tests and terror, risking everything that might occur on the bandstand, leading to moments of dawning, disaster, or both. He still harbored resentment after all these years. But he'd learned his lessons well, treating musicians in bands he eventually led the same way.

Dizzy was much more straightforward, effusive, and a lot less unpredictable. He had a joyousness that was apparent when he played and with his frolicking about on gigs, in contrast to Bird who planted himself solidly into the floor, remaining perfectly still, except when sounds burst from his saxophone, going airborne.

Miles visited Dizzy frequently at his home in Queens. His wife, Lorraine, was reserved but pleasant and welcoming. She made a point of keeping Dizzy on the straight and narrow. It was a known fact that none of his musician friends would be allowed to set foot in the house unless she was satisfied that they were not of questionable character. And that applied specifically to Charles Parker Jr. Miles though was always welcomed into their home. She saw him as a well-mannered young man, always smartly dressed and well spoken. And he was very careful never to utter that four-syllable word, a frequent visitor to his vocabulary.

"You need to listen to Pops!" Dizzy insisted.

"He's still playing what he was twenty years ago."

"Don't sleep on Pops. If it wasn't for what he did, you, me, and everybody coming after him would still be swallowing our own spit."

"I can't get with all that clowning."

"Forget his shenanigans. Once he puts that horn in his mouth, it's great gettin' up mornin'."

"But I'm looking to wake up hearing a different sound in my head, like you and Roy did."

"That's why I said you got to go through 'West End Blues' to ever hear what your voice is gonna be."

"I've listened to it. But I'm not feeling where I fit in."

"Then you ain't listened to it enough. At the beginning, you get Pops's fanfare, like he's saying 'wake up, I'm here.' No horn player was ever that bodacious, stepping out on his own like that. It was Pops playing his own version of 'Reveille.' So, between 'Reveille' and the day-is-done sound of 'Taps' is where the rest of us find out where we live."

"And what about me?"

"It ain't my place to say. But between daybreak and nightfall, you might find your place sometime around dusk."

That time arrived for Miles, without having any idea what he was about to hear. Freddie Freeloader told the story, since he happened to be the one bartending at the Royal Roost that night in the fall of 1948.

Miles was playing with Bird's quintet. The tune was "A Night in Tunisia," with Bird's solo at high pitched, bee-buzzing speed, notes chasing one another in every direction. Miles, using a mute, played at a slower, quieter pace, and for the first time he could hear his sound inside and outside of Bird's, not in a dead heat but with space to hear the difference. Shit! He'd discovered his own way of playing with Bird. He played so much saxophone, there was almost too much to ponder. But by playing less, Miles left enough evidence to wonder about.

*   *   *

Miles considered all this from his Ferrari, parked near 1580 Broadway, the old address of the now-defunct Royal Roost. What a time that was. Coming to New York in 1944, consumed with Bird, Dizzy, 52nd Street, but not so much with attending Juilliard—the only reason his parents agreed to support him. It wasn't long before he realized the location of his real education.

These fond memories were much on his mind as he looked forward to a dinner with Clark Terry. Over the years, Miles came to understand the reasons why many folks misread Clark's ever-present smile. Behind it was a steely resolve. He joked but he did not play. And it could be dangerous for anyone not to grasp the difference. Having known each other for so long, their conversation was relaxed and lively, trading stories of their youths in St. Louis and East St. Louis.

"You remember the first time we met?" Miles asked.

"In fact, it was the second time that you got my attention."

"The first time you blew me off."

"Yeah. I was distracted by some fine young ladies."

"It took a while for you to take me seriously."

"You were so skinny, I didn't think you had the stamina, let alone the energy to play a horn."

"My time with B's band gave me stamina and the thick skin I needed."

"B would stay on your back to see if you had the spine to take it."

"I remember you having big fun watching."

"That was part of your education."

"And I learned."

"And look how you ended up. At the top of your game with a fine lady."

"That's what they tell me."

"About both?"

"Yeah. But I'm suspicious of muthafuckas telling me how well I'm doing."

"Does that include me?"

"Only if you have to ask."

"Fuck you, Miles." They both laughed.

"How's Frances?"

"She's all right."

"Glad to hear it." Miles stiffened.

"There any reason why you shouldn't be?"

"I was just asking, Miles."

"What've you heard?"

"Where're you taking this?"

"You oughta know. You started it."

"Miles, we go back a long way. I'm always interested in how things are with you."

"We just spent two fuckin' hours doing that."

"Miles, I don't wanna get in your business."

"You already in it."

"I've heard some things."

"Like what?"

"Just that, you know what they say: If you hit a woman, you've already lost the argument and probably the woman too."

Miles jumped up from the table incensed. "Muthafucka! You telling me what to do?"

"I'm saying this as a friend."

"And I'm saying, you better stay the fuck away from me!" Miles stormed out of the restaurant, the patrons staring in horror. But before reaching the door, he hesitated, hearing Clark.

"I love you too, Miles."

Without turning around, he heard in Clark's voice how much he regretted the painful words exchanged between them, knowing they couldn't be taken back. He continued out of the restaurant, needing to vent the anger converging in him from two directions: anger with himself for hitting Frances and with Clark for knowing what he had done.

*   *   *

Frances was as alarmed to hear Lena Horne's voice on the phone as she was by the invitation to her home for coffee—and the quality of her enunciation and remarkable intonation. Hers was a sound of unapologetic assertion of herself. She was not to be messed with.

They'd first met when Miles took her to Horne's apartment for a party on the Upper West Side of Manhattan. On another occasion, she went to a party alone when he had a gig out of town. Horne attended the opening night of *West Side Story*, and came backstage afterward to lavish praise on her performance. Frances saw her perform in person at the Waldorf Astoria nightclub when Miles took her, earlier in the year. The show was a revelation. Horne sang words into steam with heat from her throat, and had a snarl in her voice that Frances had not seen in the movies: *Day out-day in / I needn't tell you how my days begin / When I awake with a tingle / One possibility in view* ... Lena awakens the lyrics from sleep without warning, baring her teeth in a tiger's grin, grinding words into grains of truth with fire in her eyes, burning with defiance, jutting out her chin, sashaying her hips and shoulders in a tight-fitting gown. Then her voice would soften in a quiet and well-kept way.

Frances was intimidated too. She waited until Miles was playing out of town to reply to the invitation. She left the elevator, turned down a hallway. Lena was waiting at her apartment door in a bulky turtleneck sweater, capri pants with hair flat against her scalp. Entrancing, she greeted Frances with an embrace, who noticed a wariness in Lena's eyes. Her nose, a narrow bridge of bone and a beautiful bauble of flesh at the tip, was extraordinary.

39

Frances sat on a couch in front of a coffee table and waited for Lena to bring in the coffee. This was the first time she was in Lena's presence without a crowd of people. She was nervous and began to shiver. Lena brought in a coffee pot, two mugs, and cream and sugar on a tray. She placed them on the table, sat down next to Frances, and poured the drinks. They blew into the mugs to cool it. Lena turned to Frances. Her face was brimming with curiosity.

"I've wanted to have you over since I saw you in *West Side Story*."

"You have?" Frances asked, surprised.

"I'm always interested how Negro women in show business are doing, who've come after me."

"You've been someone all of us have looked up to."

"How much do you think has changed?"

"Not as much as any of us would like."

"What about for you, personally?"

"I was fortunate to get an opportunity very young. Performing with the Paris Opera Ballet at eighteen and my years touring with Katherine Dunham."

"You, Julie Belafonte, Josephine Premice, and, of course, Eartha Kitt came up under Dunham. What was that like?" Lena asked.

"It was my finishing school for everything I did after."

"What did you think of Dunham?"

Frances added cream and sugar to her coffee. She wanted to choose her words carefully. "She pushed me beyond where I thought I could go."

Lena leaned closer to Frances like she was about to share a secret. "I've heard she could be difficult."

"She could be. But I understood. She knew if we became complacent our performance would suffer." Frances noticed that Lena frowned, perhaps hoping for a response that wasn't obvious.

"Just like you, I know something about being 'the first.' Did you feel under any pressure?"

"Not at all. My parents believed in me. They told me there was nothing I couldn't achieve. So, when the Paris Opera Ballet chose me, I have to say, it didn't come as a complete surprise."

Lena snickered. "Some might say you're very full of yourself."

"Only when I danced."

"Did other dancers resent you?"

Frances blinked in surprise. "Not as far as I know. Julie and Josephine are two of my best friends."

Lena stared at her and took a sip of coffee.

"You're fortunate to have women friends you trust. That's been rare for me. What do you talk about? The men in your lives?"

"They're famous. They get talked about enough as it is. We don't need to do that when we get together."

Lena sighed. "So, if not them, what?"

"We made a pact never to share what we talk about."

"That's wise," Lena said, nodding. "But how do you deal with the rumors that follow you because of the men you're with?"

"Knowing most are not true makes them fun to talk about."

Lena's attention drifted briefly.

"I wish the rumors about me had been fun ... But I hear you're getting married," Lena said, wanting to change the subject.

"Yes, I am," Frances said. Her shoulders tightened. She wondered: was that the reason for the invitation?

"Congratulations." Lena raised her mug.

"Thank you."

"Your parents must be pleased."

"They always are, once they know I'm doing something I really want."

"I've always had difficulty figuring out what 'wanting' and 'really wanting' mean," Lena said wistfully.

"Aren't you doing what you always really wanted to do?" Frances asked.

"That can change. My mother always 'wanted' to be a star. And when that didn't happen, she tried to make me one."

"So, being a singer wasn't something you really wanted to do?"

"Not at first. It took a while for me to really want to be in show business—as much as my mother did."

"Do you regret all you've had to do to get where you're a sensation in night clubs just about everywhere?"

"I've had my regrets." A silence swelled between them. "You were fortunate," Lena said, finally, "to have had parents that didn't live through your success."

"I was."

"I told just about everyone I know to see *West Side Story*, especially, to see you, but then I heard you left the show. Why?"

Frances shifted uncomfortably on the couch. "I needed to take some time to sort out a few things. I have a son who's been staying with my parents and I've got to make arrangements for him to come to New York." She took a breath, relaxing a hand gripping her knee.

"To raise a child and remain a creative person is difficult. I know from bitter experience. Do you plan to return to the show?"

"Getting married and having my son with us . . ." a memory flashed in her head—back-arching high kicks, quick snap back of head and leg, flamenco foot chatter, whiplashing skirt, cutting the air to shreds, rapid-fire hand claps, *good-to-be-white-in-Am-er-ee-ca*!

"Frances?"

". . . Oh, it's just that there's a lot to manage," she said, coming back from her other self.

"It sounds like you and Miles are devoted to each other."

Frances hesitated. "Yes, we are."

"You know, when you came to my party without Miles, he called to see if you were enjoying yourself."

"What did you tell him?"

"I told him if he wanted to know if you were enjoying yourself, he should talk to you. But he hung up."

"Is that why you invited me here? To tell me that?"

"I've known Miles a long time. I know it's no surprise to you that he can behave like a potentate. My reasons were selfish. I have more than a few years on you. And I was curious how much of myself when I was your age I see in you."

"So, what do you see?"

"You appear more grounded than I was. When I saw your performance, my impression was that you possessed a readiness that's likely always been there. When I was young, I was hardly ready. Totally confused. Didn't know my ass from my elbow." Lena snorted. "You weren't under siege the way I was—a star in Hollywood. That was unthinkable for our people. We played maids and underlings to white folks. That's what they did to us. As a so-called 'first,' I had responsibilities: representing our people, doing right by them, and making them proud. That was my job on top of entertaining. Many of our colored folk who preceded me in the movies thought I believed I was too good to play the roles they couldn't afford to turn down. The first real part, promised to me by Louis B. Mayer, was Julie, the mulatto in *Showboat*. That went to my dear friend Ava Gardner whose skin was darkened and her voice dubbed. The only role I was ever to play was Lena Horne. So, I took the role as a spokesman for our people in the fight for equal rights and I was accused of being unpatriotic and a communist on the one hand, a sellout on the other. The former prevented me from getting work for several years. I did things I'm not proud of, demeaning myself to get back into the good graces of people I didn't even respect. And I just about destroyed my marriage. I fell off the cliff of my own life . . . So, here I am over forty, making an effort to climb back up to myself."

"You think I gave up," Frances said, not looking directly at Lena.

"I'll only say this. I've always undermined myself when I've gotten caught up in why someone did me wrong, instead paying attention to the wrong done to me. That only I can do something about."

Frances walked to the elevator. Lena called out to her. "You think we ought to make a pact, not to share with anyone what we talked about?"

"Only about the lies we told each other that we said were true," Frances said. She heard Lena's laughter even after she closed the door. But Frances didn't think what she said was a laughing matter.

*   *   *

Miles didn't want to get past what those fuckin' cops did, especially the one he didn't see, coldcocking him from behind. He knew he had taken some of it out on Frances, but couldn't help himself. Cutting himself some slack was bullshit! He knew you can't bullshit a bullshitter, 'cause he was one of 'em. He'd been helping himself to a great many things belonging to Frances without asking permission. He'd fessed up to it, but he was unable or had just refused to do anything more than that . . .

When he was in one of his "fuck it" moods, he'd go to a movie to chill. He loved to go to the grindhouses on 42nd Street. Its seediness attracted him. At night, Forty-Deuce was reeling like a drunk feeling no pain who by morning was hung over. It had everything he'd heard about growing up in East St. Louis and across the river in St. Louis: pimps, hos, druggies, freaks, hustlers, punks, gangsters, and undercover cops. These were the muthafuckas hanging out in jazz clubs. After he got caught up in shit beyond the clubs, he discovered none of it was fun and games. A deadly hurting could be put on him if he wasn't careful, and even if he was. But he had a higher opinion of the guttersnipes and lowlifes of Forty-Deuce than the tired, saditty-ass, bullshit middle-class Negro world of his parents.

The flick Miles checked out was *Some Like It Hot*. George Raft was in it. He played gangsters in movies of the thirties and forties. He was born in Hell's Kitchen, one of the roughest sections of

Manhattan, and had to fight and do whatever it took to survive. It made him perfect for roles as a gangster. Miles dug the way Raft carried himself. You could never tell what he was thinking: his face in a deep freeze, slicked-back hair like a skull cap, and dressed in tailored suits, looking like they had been waiting for him even before he bought them. He also danced a mean tango, his right arm a tightened belt around his partner's waist, and his feet in an ice-skating slide across the dance floor. The movie was about two bass players in the 1920s, forced to split and disguise themselves in drag after witnessing gangsters ice some rivals in a St. Valentine's Day–style massacre. Miles wasn't interested whether the musicians would end up getting offed. It was a fuckin' comedy. He was more interested in who was in it. George Raft had a small part, but the main stars were Marilyn Monroe, Tony Curtis, and Jack Lemmon. Curtis and Lemmon were pretty good, especially Curtis, and Monroe was okay. Lemmon wasn't that realistic, imitating how a woman walked in high heels. He moved like he was about to topple on his ass. Plus, his legs were too masculine, with calf muscles the size of oranges, not like Frances whose dancer's legs were lean and beautifully shaped from ankle, calf, to thigh. He knew that wasn't the point. The audience was in on the joke. No one watching the movie would believe Lemmon and Curtis were convincing, but everybody on screen did. That was funny, but what really intrigued Miles was the contrast between Tony Curtis and Marilyn. He thought Curtis was sexier than Monroe. He had a sensuous mouth and soft features going for him, like Elvis. Everything about Monroe was exaggerated. She was working overtime to appeal to what men wanted to see: a male fantasy of a big-breasted blonde, but nothing beyond that except a good fuck. Monroe played that role too many times. She was in drag a lot more than Tony Curtis, who didn't play an idea of a woman as an outta control, showing-too-much-titty, ass-shaking spectacle of herself. In other words, a ho! Curtis imitated a woman but was not too showy, doing more with less, like a piano player who's stingy with notes. And that was sexy like a muthafucka!

For Miles, the best part of the movie was the ending, where this sucka, with a mouth so big you could put a billiard ball in it, wants to marry Jack Lemmon, thinking he's a woman. When Lemmon says, "I can't marry you, I'm a man," the guy says, "Well, nobody's perfect."

Miles really dug that. If a man who somebody thought was a woman wasn't perfect, why would he, who was a man that wasn't perfect, be dogged by muthafuckas with their asses on their shoulders who want him to be different from what he already was—not perfect.

*   *   *

Frances saw Miles was in a foul mood when he returned to the apartment from his dinner. She braced herself. He closed the door and stopped a few feet into the apartment.

"How was your dinner with Clark?" she asked, cautiously.

"Is that who you've been talking to?"

"About what?"

"Like you don't know."

"Miles, why don't you start at the beginning of what you want to talk to me about."

"I'm talking 'bout you telling other people what's going on with us."

"Why don't we sit down."

"I'm fine where I am."

She went into the living room and sat down on a couch.

"Who are these other people?" she asked.

"You tell me."

"You're the only one I talk to about us."

He joined her on the couch, but at a distance. "I told you how bad I felt about what I did."

"You've said that before."

"This time I mean it."

"Miles, you always end up doing what you want to do." Her eyes widened. She surprised herself.

"If I do, what about you? You must be doing what you wanna do. We're together, ain't we?"

She shifted her weight on the couch and looked at him directly. "I was hoping you would change."

He moved closer and placed a hand on her thigh. "Do I frighten you that much?"

She heard a plea in his voice.

"Not always," she said.

"When I do, I always hope you won't leave."

"I guess we're both stuck."

"What's that mean?"

"When you make me afraid, I feel you're just as afraid of yourself."

He jumped up from the couch. "Where the fuck you get that from?"

"Something I've been thinking."

"Some thoughts should be silent and not spoken."

She flinched. He saw it in her face.

"We've been good together, haven't we?"

"Some of the time."

"I'm gonna do better about the other times."

"What about the cocaine?"

"I got it under control."

"Under control, but not stopped."

"We ain't gonna go through that again, are we?"

"No, not we, Miles, me."

She considered the steady gaze passing between them, seeing that he looked as exhausted as she was. She touched the side of his face.

"Miles, you once told me that music was your way of praying. But I don't understand why you only want to hear your prayer and not mine."

He bent his head and pressed the palm of his hand firmly against his forehead. Short bursts of breath came from his mouth. He got to his feet, reached for her hand and pulled her up from the couch. In bed, she tried to speak, but words choked in her throat. She heard his sobs. And their bodies, juiced together in sweat, finally quieted. Near dawn, Frances was awakened by the sound of pounding, knowing immediately it was Miles punching the heavy bag.

*   *   *

Miles, still parked in front of Bop City, roused himself from his reverie. He disliked the name of the venue for its predictability. He preferred its former name: the Royal Roost. The words signified the highest order among all the cats who hung out to play and challenge each other. He drove around the corner to 52nd Street. Gone was the greased lightning reflecting off the street from the clubs that were joined at the hip: The Onyx, The Spotlight, Club Samoa, Club Downbeat, Club Carousel, and the Three Deuces. Anyone looking down from the heights of Rockefeller Center or any of the

other skyscrapers hovering over the clubs would see lights burning from marquees. He tuned up the volume in his ears, hearing
again the gravelly voice of Symphony Sid and musicians playing at
frantic tempos that blew open the doors. Now there wasn't even a
flickering ember of the former fire. That night in 1948 at the Royal
Roost was a moment of truth for him, providing evidence that he
could carry his own weight and could join the party without an
invitation. It also brought back the stranglehold of anger against
Bird that he finally recognized in the four years since his death.

Damn, he thought. It was so unlike him to dwell on the past. He
couldn't forget Bird stuffing himself until the seams holding his life
together came apart. Bird possessed an incandescent fire, lighting
up the world. But that did not prove enough to save him. Nothing
was ever enough. The surge of notes streaming from his horn left
behind too much for those who revered him to fully take in. Miles's
compression of fewer notes, sharpened whistle-like through his
trumpet, left enough evidence of his oncoming hunger. He looked
down at where Bird had landed, as if from a seesaw. But he didn't
expect to slam into the ground and, like Bird, be unable to lift
himself from the depths of his own tragic magic.

*   *   *

Miles hadn't returned. Frances was stretched out on the floor,
back against the wall, still wearing her ballet slippers and tights.
She smiled and her jaw tightened. The previous spring, she'd run
into Eartha Kitt on Fifth Avenue, near the north end of Central
Park. From her beginnings with the Katherine Dunham Dance
Company, Eartha had made a stunning debut in the *New Faces of
1952* Broadway musical revue which ran for nearly a year before
becoming a movie. She had become a scintillating international
chanteuse, compared to the petite dynamo Edith Piaf with her
trembling, big-throated voice and to Marlene Dietrich for her
provocative sexual allure. Wearing dark glasses, Eartha didn't
notice Frances walking toward her. She wore beige leather slacks,
a matching wraparound bathrobe-style jacket, a blue velvet head-
wrap, and loafers. The slacks didn't entrap her legs, and were loose
enough to reveal their fabulous shape.

"Hi Kitty," Frances said, a name used by those who knew
her well.

Eartha stopped, pulling her dark glasses down to eye level. She stared warily at Frances, attentive to the legs below the hem of her skirt. "Still have those great legs, Franny. But mine are insured by Lloyd's of London."

They embraced. Eartha's face was a marvel—honey-brushed skin, smooth cheeks over barely visible bones, a strong curvaceous jaw line, a tight slit of a mouth, incapable of preventing whatever she chose to come out of it. No one looked like her.

"You look great," Frances said.

"I wouldn't say that. You caught me without my face on."

Frances thought that even without makeup her beauty was evident.

"How are things with you and Miles?"

"We're fine."

"So. What are you doing?" Eartha asked, emphasizing "you."

"I'm teaching dance at the Graham school."

Eartha raised her eyebrows, both shaped like the blade of a knife.

"They're lucky to have you. I don't know about the other way around."

"What are you up to?" Frances asked, not wanting to get into that.

"I'm singing in the Persian Room at the Plaza, where I'm staying."

"That's great."

"Why don't you come and have a drink?"

They were half a block away from the hotel and Eartha stopped.

"Wait for me in front of the hotel," she said.

"Why?"

"Just do it."

She stopped at the hotel entrance and turned around. Eartha reached into her purse and took out something that might have been a coin. She tossed it about a foot in front of her. She lifted her chest and shoulders repeatedly and stared at the sidewalk. She took a leap over the coin, landing on her left foot, and shouting, "One, two," balancing herself. "It's been a while since I've done this, Franny," she said, her breathing a bit labored. She took another leap, landing on the foot of the right leg, "Three," then jumping onto the left foot, "four, five, six," and then the right, "Seven," and onto the left, "eight, nine," and then landing on the right foot, "Ten."

Frances watched the incredulous pedestrians moving out of the way. Eartha stood in front of her, beaming like a seven-year-old.

"Hopscotching on one leg, Kitty. You're too much. "

"No. I'm not enough. Come on. Let's have that drink."

She was accosted by guests wanting autographs and basked in the attention. The concierge rushed over, asking the excited fans not to bother the hotel's special guest. He apologized profusely, but Eartha waved it off. They went into the hotel lounge. They were seated and Eartha ordered two glasses of Dom Perignon.

"What brought all that on?" Frances asked.

"That was Eartha Mae. I left her in South Carolina. Sometimes, I find myself wanting her back."

"You played hopscotch in South Carolina?"

"No. I didn't learn how until I came to New York. Girls teased me because I'd never seen it before. But I was a quick study and outdid them all. The same thing happened when I auditioned for Dunham. I watched the other dancers, memorized what they did, and was offered a scholarship."

Frances was briefly lost in thought.

"Since I was trained in ballet, I was out of my element when I first joined Dunham. We always warmed up with the drummers. And there were a lot of sharp elbows thrown around with the tested dancers getting in front of the line. That first group set the tone, moving to the changing rhythms of the drummers. Once reaching the opposite wall, they watched, arms folded, their mouths turned up, letting newcomers like myself know the low regard they had for us. I was just thinking about what you said about learning to hopscotch. Even after I moved up to the front of the line, I never wanted to subject less-confident dancers to the humiliation I felt."

"That's so much like you, Franny. I wanted to turn those dismissive looks into grudging respect, and rub it in, just like I did to those girls who thought they were better than me."

"I have to say, I admire that," Frances said.

"That's one of the reasons why I left Dunham. She didn't always treat us well. She was such a diva."

Frances stretched her eyes wide.

"Don't even say it, Franny."

"I didn't say a word."

"You don't have to. I can see what you're thinking."

Frances couldn't stop a smile from worming across her mouth.

"While you're busy seeing what I think," she said, "I'm remembering all the rumors I heard that you'd outgrown the Company and wanted to move on. That was right before I joined."

"I'm glad you said 'joined.' I've heard people say you replaced me. No reflection on you, Franny, but no one could've replaced me."

"Absolutely, Kitty. You were and are irreplaceable."

Eartha threw her head back, opened her cavernous mouth, and boomed out laughter Frances thought was worthy of Tallulah Bankhead. But there was bitterness around the edges.

"Franny, you are priceless. You're so careful with your words, like you never are when you dance. You take no prisoners."

To Frances's ear, Eartha talked the way she sang. Her voice was a hum of words. The waiter arrived with the champagne. They raised their glasses.

"To you, Franny, to what you do best." They clinked glasses.

"Thank you for that, Kitty."

Eartha sipped her champagne, leveled her eyes at Frances, who felt a sting of hostility.

"Since you're thankful for my toast, I should tell you that last week I appeared on *What's My Line?* as the mystery guest. And I stumped the panel. You're a mystery guest who's always stumped me."

"What do you mean?"

"Franny, you've always been a welcomed guest at the party, but it's a mystery to me how you don't appreciate how great a gift that is."

"I still don't understand."

Eartha held out her hand. "You came into this world in the palm of a hand." She balled up her fingers. "I was born in a fist. It was all there for you. I didn't know there was a 'there.' Dirt was how I was treated. It didn't occur to me that dirt is the earth, like my name, that grows things. How long do you think your 'earth' is going to be there, before dirt will be the only way you're treated?"

Frances's stomach clenched. "I don't believe that's my fate."

"We're alike in that way, Franny. Rita Hayworth once said every man she ever went to bed with wanted to have sex with Rita Hayworth, not Margarita Carmen Cansino. I want to believe it won't always be that way. Until then, I'll continue to play at being Eartha Kitt and you'll still play at being content."

Sweat tingled hot on Frances' skin. Eartha saw her mouth twitch. "I'm sorry," she said. "You don't deserve that, especially coming from me."

"I have to go," Frances said, draining the glass of champagne and getting up.

"That's you all right, Franny. Going, going, gone. It's just in the wrong direction."

"So much for being sorry," she said, fed up with listening to Kitty.

"Finally, some righteous anger. Dunham said that's what you lacked. You're just not cruel enough."

"That definitely works for you."

"It works, at least, as well as you taking shit."

Frances turned to leave. "Goodbye, Kitty."

"I don't get you, Franny."

"That's because I got there ahead of you."

"Let me know what you find."

*   *   *

Miles jerked awake. He looked around—still parked in front of Bop City. Before nodding off, he'd been thinking of a night in 1953. He was living in Detroit, playing periodically at various clubs. It was there, one rainy night, that Max Roach and Clifford Brown played at a club called the Crystal Lounge. During a particular set, Max and Brownie sent those present into such a frenzy, it was difficult to quell. What happened next was recounted by many who claimed to have been there. When the set ended, Brownie came off the bandstand and Miles walked in from the rain outside. He asked Brownie for his trumpet, reached into his pocket, took out his mouthpiece, and played "My Funny Valentine." After he finished, the only sound accompanying the silence in the club was the sound of the downpour. He then took his mouthpiece out of the horn, gave Brownie his trumpet and without a word, walked out of the club.

Many disputed numerous details of the story. As expected, Freddie Freeloader was one of them.

I happened to be in Detroit that night, working as Max and Brownie's bodyguard. You gotta watch your back in Detroit, otherwise you could end up on it . . . The 411 on what really went down is that Miles comes in out of the rain, drenched and a little shaky. He had his trumpet with him, but not his mouthpiece. Fortunately, Brownie had an extra one and let Miles borrow it. Now, any words I come up with that's close to the actual words Miles might have used to explain what did happen would be lame 'cause Miles don't ever talk about his music. But since I don't play, all I can do is talk about what I don't do. So, I'm gonna put the words he didn't say in my mouth . . . My funny valentine is a gift sent to someone I know and don't know.

But both make up my better self—when I smile with my heart that's laughable, especially when photographable . . . Now, my mouth is weak when I desperately need to speak. Is it smart to say, care for me, but if you can't for me, stay with me, my valentine stay . . . Those words came to me listening to Miles play "My Funny Valentine." And if you don't like it, we can take it outside.

Miles played ballads reluctantly, precisely because he loved them. What he remembered most about that night in Detroit was the loss of his mouthpiece and what its disappearance said about the depth of the hole he was digging for himself.

*   *   *

People called his performance at the July 1955 Newport Jazz Festival a resurrection, and he took issue with that. It was said that he played a stunning solo on "'Round Midnight" that afternoon. He didn't think it was elevated above other solos he'd played of Monk's composition. His mind was on the not unexpected death of Bird a few months earlier. He was found at the Stanhope Hotel. The coroner who performed the autopsy believed the body to be of a man nearly twice his actual age. He was thirty-four years old. His passing cast a dark cloud over the entire festival. That far-reaching cloud turned sinister a month later with the lynching of Emmett Till in Mississippi. That unrecognizable boy was fourteen years old. A horrific photograph of his bloated face appeared in *Jet* magazine for the world to see. A few weeks later, Miles's quintet played a gig at a Baltimore club. He felt a surge of rage that Bird's greediness had quickened the time that took him down, and rage in response to the hatred that crushed the life out of a Black boy. One of the tunes on the playlist was "'Round Midnight." Miles nearly passed on it. But then, bending his head, he pointed his trumpet down into the quiet night of its mute over a mic lowered waist high. What occurred at that Baltimore club was one of the few events that Freddie Freeloader had to be begged to recount.

I drove down to Baltimore from my hometown in Philly with some buddies of mine. In one way, I wish I hadn't been there. In another, there's nowhere else I wanted to be. It's like, what's good for the soul can break your heart . . . How do you ask Miles to play "'Round Midnight" when he may not have the notes to give Bird and this broken child . . . He plays, as he squeezes away the sting in his eyes. Trane murmurs, slow and not too low. For Miles, it's 'round midnight, with no more suppertime or sundown for Emmett and Bird, one giving so much for not very long, the other having little time to give at all ... Red plays in the key of touch and go lightly. Paul hugs the bass for memories that rumble 'round midnight. Philly Joe stirs up sand with his brushes. All three cornered in a rhythm of amen. Miles returns to his voice—not having the heart to withstand those memories—saying "my heart's still with you and midnight knows it too," as Trane foghorns in prayer: "what needs mending, does it mean our love is ending? Emmett and Bird, you're not out of my heart or out of my mind." Miles, a quiver in his heart, takes flight 'round midnight. The angels, Emmett and Bird, sing in his sound—with Red, Paul, and Philly Joe, old midnight comes back around, feeling sad and still it really gets bad and midnight knows it too ...

*   *   *

Miles shook his head out of the long-gone days. The "Kind of Blue" album had been released only eight days before and he was mostly satisfied with what the group had accomplished. Those cops fucked it up. He drove downtown to the 30th Street Studio where the album was recorded. He stared at the building. Familiar to him, he was always struck by how nondescript what had been a Greek Orthodox church was. The structure had an angled roof and half-moon trappings surrounding the windows, identifying it as a former house of worship. From where he stood, the Empire State Building was visible. Miles and Bill Evans, replacing Wynton Kelly for the session, had sketched out some ideas beforehand. The group talked about the first chorus of each tune and the order. Miles didn't usually like to revisit music after it was recorded. But he revisited the time with Cannonball, Bill, and Trane, who were leaving after the completion of the album ...

*   *   *

Cannonball. My man. Always shows up. He could chill Miles out, helping him to calm the fuck down. He was a man of full stature with ample weight and no need to throw it around. He was unflappable among musicians who could be unmerciful, trading insults as readily as they took a breath. Like Ellington, he loved the taste

53

of words in his mouth. He turned trash to treasure, and had folks wondering if he was raising you up or putting you down ...

*   *   *

Miles remembered hearing Bill Evans the first time at the Village Vanguard and was surprised how he was carried away by the uninterrupted ebb and flow of his playing. Evans never played ahead of himself, but stayed in the moment. There was a quiet intensity to his playing that didn't shower the piano with notes to prove his virtuosity. This quality was in line with Miles's belief in using fewer notes and filling the spaces with silence. When he looked up at the end of the set, he was startled to see Miles standing by the side of the piano.

"What are you doing when you finish here?" Miles asked.

"You mean after the gig tonight?"

"No, man. I'm talking about when your date is over here."

"I don't know."

"Well, I'm forming a sextet. So let me know what you decide." He turned and left before giving Evans an opportunity to respond one way or the other.

There was grumbling about Miles hiring a white musician when there were so many deserving Negro musicians not being hired by white bands. Miles wasn't fazed. Anyone who didn't like it could suck on a fuckin' butt and hug a nut. He riled up Negro musicians even more by publicly praising a white musician like Bobby Hackett as one of his favorite trumpet players over Clark Terry, his homeboy from St. Louis. Neither did he spare his bandmates with off-the-wall opinions and brief, unclear directions. "Do what I don't say, not what I say, when I don't do what I do say." This was too much for his pianist, Red Garland, who left the band. Not to give the impression of prejudice, Miles wasted no time probing Bill with scalpel-like precision wherever he saw an opening.

"Damn, Bill," he said with a seriousness that couldn't be mistaken, "I didn't tell you when you joined the sextet, you have to fuck the band." Bill looked at the other band members who averted their eyes. Dumbfounded, he turned to Miles, looking for some sign that he was bullshitting. But none came.

Bill looked dejected. "I'm sorry, Miles, but I don't think I can do that."

Miles's deadpan cracked open, and along with the others, broke into high-fiving laughter. "All right, Bill. Forget it."

Miles grew close to Bill, as a kindred spirit who pushed the band into uncharted territory. He began to notice that, occasionally, when Bill was away from the piano, he would drift. He knew exactly what was happening, as did Trane, Red, Philly Joe, and Paul. They had all been there when the "white bitch" heroin took them down. Miles found out the Negro woman Bill was living with tried, unsuccessfully, to get him to cut the bitch loose. He tried to imagine what he would say to him.

"Does the bitch fuck that good?"

"It's better than fucking the band."

"You never know."

"I'm already spoken for."

"Tell her to go fuck herself."

"I already tried."

"You don't mind doing a three way with the band, your Negro woman, and that ho you running with in the street?"

"She's got my nose open too wide."

"How long do you think you can go on like this?"

"Until I can't."

"I hear you. The tragic magic is the bitch that'll let you break your heart."

But Miles couldn't bring himself to have that conversation with Bill. At the end of the recording session at the 30th Street Studio in April, Bill told Miles he was leaving the band.

"Did I get under your skin too much, joking about you being white?"

"You didn't mess with me any more than the rest of the guys, just different, that's all."

"You know I hired you no matter what any muthafucka said."

"I know that, Miles. We're cool. But if I'm out of place no matter where I am, I have to be on my own ..."

*   *   *

From the beginning, Trane didn't have a lotta mouth, except when his horn was in it. Folks slept on Trane. He was thick bodied, dressed a little shabby and, if truth be told, "country." Armani wasn't his thing. And if you checked him up close, you'd notice, from time to time, the muthafucka didn't have on no socks. After hiring him the first time, he knew Trane had a gorilla on his back. Miles wasn't having it and fired him. But Trane cleaned himself up and returned like hellfire. You could see the fierceness in his eyes. You also saw a kindness that made you want to make sure he ate regularly, and do whatever else you could do for him, 'cause he had the goods and was ready to get down in the hard love and grit like nobody's business. Miles knew Trane would be leaving the band after the gig at Birdland and knew he was gonna miss him. But he had his own version of "every goodbye ain't gone" before he left.

"I know I never said that much to you."

"You didn't have to. You showed me, in a few words, to let my playing do the talking," Trane said.

"You played yourself into a lotta corners, but found a way out of one and into another."

"I appreciate that you allowed me to stretch out."

"You stretched out all right, like you yawned yourself into somethin' you probably can't explain but don't need to."

"Well, I do want to thank you, Miles."

"You don't need to chew on that no more."

"I mean when you hired me back."

"Yeah. When you was doing more nodding than yawning."

A silence wedged between them.

"Well," Miles said, "since we always made space for silence in the band, why don't we leave it there."

When Miles felt no need to keep up a front, there was no way around it: He loved that muthafucka...

*   *   *

Given the shit that went down with those cops earlier in the evening, the cut "So What," from the new album, was on his mind. Miles remembered he'd been in a good mood and allowed Freddie Freeloader to be present for the recording.

I told folks when I was hanging out at Birdland what a big fuckin' deal it was to be at the session. A guy in the booth called out for the first take of a tune. I was blown away when I heard the title: "Freddie Freeloader." My mind dummied up on me and I couldn't focus on the music. When they finished the take, Miles smiled at me. He don't give up many of those. So, I bowed and turned my back on him. He just about busted a gut laughing, and so did everybody else ... The next tune called out from the booth was something called "So What." Bill and Paul opened with a fingered hum on bass and a two-note piano jangle, a "let me give you a heads-up" and a "tell me more." That took them into further earfuls of conversatin' until Paul stops their head to head. He plucked about ten boom-boom-booms, as in "I think we got company," but it was cool. Miles and Cannonball overhear Paul and Bill's booms and jingles . . . Trumpet and alto play in unison, "So what!" with Miles adding and "I don't care 'bout none a that shit!" And since he don't like repeating himself, he hits a medium pitched "all right, can we get on with it," alerting Jimmy to drum them into what's about to jump off and heeding Miles with a sis-boom-bam cymbal splash, spraying everywhere. Then came the time for everybody to get dibs on the opening chatter between Paul and Bill with Jimmy and Paul rock solid underneath the bounce and roll of Miles blowin' a fine rain and a straight razor. Cannonball was all up in his jovial alto and Trane was giving everyone more than a piece of his full tenor platter of mind-grabbing sayso, getting the band to, maybe, consider that "So what" may not be the final words to everything they'd been riffing on. Howsomever, Miles signals Trane, Cannonball, and Jimmy that it's time to split, leaving Paul and Bill to return to their quiet kibitzing before the humming bass and jangling piano fade to—enough is enough . . . Now, tell me, can it get any better than that . . .

Having heard it in his head, Miles was a bit bummed out that they hadn't quite nailed it. But because of the mistakes it was pretty damn fuckin' good!

*   *   *

Miles drove further uptown to Gil's old apartment, across Manhattan to 55th Street near Fifth Avenue. They had met in the late forties. The two artists, ten years apart in age, shared an affinity for extending jazz from a quick, out-of-the-box, purposeful ensemble where everyone got a turn doing sky-scraping solos, to a larger, quieter, less-hurried unit, having its own intensity envisioned not as an end in itself but a beginning of something yet to come. Gil lived in the storage room at the back of a Chinese laundry, with few amenities other than those that mattered to him: an upright piano, a phonograph, a hotplate, a counter-sized refrigerator, a desk the size of a card table, and a few rickety chairs. The place was a hothouse for serious musicians working out ideas. He and Miles collaborated for more than a decade. Miles had his own corner at the rear of Charlie's Tavern on 55th and Seventh Avenue. In recent years, it had become a watering hole for musicians.

He and Gil would hang out there at a counter, curved like a bend in the road. Miles was enjoying his growing reputation. He sat in the back to have a better view of anyone coming in. He'd heard Malcolm X did the same when he was out in restaurants. The collaborators discussed the *Sketches of Spain* sessions, which were to begin soon. Miles noticed how little he'd changed over the years. He still had sharp, angular features. His total lack of attention to clothes amused Miles, but he had great respect for him. There was no one he knew who had such an all-consuming commitment to music. Still rail thin, he was "light in the behind," but his energy and stamina were not revealed in his physical presence.

"If you didn't come in here on a regular basis, you could be mistaken for a vagrant," Miles quipped.

"That's why I hang out with you, Miles. You give me cover."

Miles had an ease with Gil, unlike anyone else. He leaned back in his seat and frowned.

"Oh, come on, Gil! You don't need me to give you cover."

"You cover my arrangements when you bring them to life, despite my mistakes."

"It's more likely that your arrangements cover up mine."

"You're too kind, Miles," Gil said, wryly.

"Why you always wanna undercut the credit you deserve?"

"I don't want to diminish what I've done. I'm just glad I don't have to prove it in front of an audience, like you do. It's one thing to conduct an orchestra during the *Porgy and Bess* recording, but quite another to direct an eleven-piece ensemble, like I did recently at the Apollo. It was unnerving having an audience listening with my back to them, while I'm focusing on the musicians in front of me, hoping they're following my directions."

"When I do that, muthafuckas think I'm disrespecting them."

Gil shook his head.

"I don't know how you do it with people that close to you."

"It takes a lot for me to get in front of an audience," Miles said. "I'm on edge before every gig. In East St. Louis, I always played with large bands. With the Eckstine Band, I was scared shitless around all those giants, knowing I had no fuckin' idea what I was doing. They covered my ass in front of all them folks coming to hear the band. That's the only time they ever cut me any slack. And I didn't want none. Coming to New York, as much as I needed to be here, was worse than East St. Louis, 'cause in smaller ensembles on 52nd Street or in Harlem, I couldn't disappear. I willed myself not to play so bad that I'd want to disappear, but to get good enough to be fuckin' noticed."

"See Miles, that's why I got it made in the shade of a recording studio, where I don't have to worry about any of that."

"Gil, forget all I just said. It's all bullshit! I didn't take my own advice, saying more with less. I'm just shy, that's all."

They burst out laughing.

"Miles, didn't you say you were going to check out some flamenco, as part of your preparation for our Spanish recording?"

"Right. Frances finally got me to go and see a performance. It was fuckin' amazing, especially the women. What they do with their wrists, guiding fingers, hands, arms, shoulders, legs, and feet covers everything my band does, keeping time with hands, shoulders, and thighs, clapping just like Philly Joe and Paul, changing tempos, toe stomping down on top of heel stomping, easing to the soft sole of the shoeslide. They don't hold back. I ain't never seen nothing like it!"

"Sounds like you were impressed. It reminds me what you said the first time you saw Frances dance."

Miles gave Gil a wide-eyed stare.

"What're you getting at Gil?"

"I was just wondering."

"What about?"

"Frances pulled your coat to *Porgy and Bess* and now she's gotten you interested in Flamenco."

"So?"

"She'd probably enjoy coming to the recording sessions."

"You know, Gil, I need to learn how to call myself on the phone and tell myself when to shut up."

*   *   *

After years of making the rounds, there were important musical markers for Miles all over. A bit further uptown were the San Juan Hill Houses where Monk lived. His presence loomed large in Miles's creative life, and at times was a source of aggravation. Their musical differences, usually resolved, did occasionally bring them nearly to blows. Like that time at the Café Bohemia in Greenwich Village. The marquee was illuminated with huge lettering announcing the group currently appearing and Monk stopped by and sat in with the quintet, causing quite a stir, playing with his elbows. Miles spit up laughter, unable to contain himself. At the end of the set, he went out in front of the club to have a smoke. Monk followed him. A sheepish grin cracked Monk's face. Miles maintained a serious front.

"Monk, was you gonna say somethin'?"

"Why should I? You always want me to lay out when you playing."

"That's 'cause you have trouble playing behind horn players."

"If you got a problem playing in front of me, that's on you."

"Maybe playing with your elbows would help me out."

"You could be right. But that won't help you play "'Round Midnight' right, like I taught you. But you ain't learned yet."

"Monk, I remember you telling me, when I first got to New York, that getting it wrong is sometimes a good place to be."

"You listened a lot better when you didn't 'know' shit."

"I ain't never stopped listening."

"Now you think you know some shit and only listen to yourself."

"And you don't?"

Miles waited. Monk tugged at his goatee, still smiling.

"I don't let cats I play with 'know' it like you do."

"That's probably why you ain't got a band."

"You may not either. I hear rumblings."

"Like what?"

"The Trane may be leaving the station."

Miles liked that.

"You a funny muthafucka, Monk."

"And you a mean one."

"I ain't mean, I'm me."

"Same difference."

Miles frowned and sucked his teeth.

"If I'm mean, that ain't even the half of me."

"It was more than half the night you were playing here and punched Trane. He don't deserve to be treated like that."

"He didn't deserve treating himself like he was doing. He was nodding out on the bandstand. I went through that and watched Red, Paul, and Philly Joe go through it. And Trane hurt me the most 'cause he's one of the best of us. It made me as mad as I was with Bird, and as mad as he was with me. I wanted to hit somethin', so it was him."

"That don't justify it."

"That ain't what I was doin'."

"Sounds like you are."

"Yeah, well, one thing about you, Monk, as strange as you are, you ain't never separated how you sound from the way you are ... Like the time we was jammin' at a studio and you did some silly shit, going in my pockets while I'm soloing, taking my cigarettes and matches."

"That's 'cause I was lookin for a tune of mine you took and played all wrong."

"Tell me somethin' I don't already know, Monk."

"Bye-Ya."

Miles shook his head, and turning to go back inside, heard Monk walking away, humming the melody after he said the name of that damn tune he wrote.

*   *   *

Miles had lost track of time. The morning light was beginning to slice into the night. He should've headed home. But not yet. He'd found himself in the 80s on the Upper West Side—thinking of Bill Evans who lived on 83rd Street. There was a phone booth on the same block, giving him a clear view of the building and Bill's third floor apartment window facing the street. A light was on behind a curtain. He dialed the number he used frequently during the time Bill was a member of the sextet.

"Hello," came Bill's voice.   Miles said nothing. "Is that you, Miles?"

"Yeah."

"You're the only one I know who's silent when I answer the phone."

"You always understood that."

"What's going on, Miles?"

"I got into a hassle with some fuckin' cops tonight in front of Birdland."

"Are you alright?"

"I'm riding around in my Ferrari to find out."

Bill pulled back the curtain and saw Miles in the phone booth.

"What about you, Bill?"

"I'm doing what I always do."

"When I first saw you, you looked like Clark Kent. You know, the slicked-back hair, the glasses, the suit and tie. After listening to you, I knew you weren't no Clark Kent and didn't need that other funny-looking suit."

"I'm glad it was a case of mistaken identity."

"How's Peri?"

"She left."

"Did she want to leave or need to?"

"I understand why she needed to leave."

"I used to believe wanting and needing weren't the same thing. Bird showed me different. Whatever he wanted, he got to needing. It became the same thing. I thought that'd never happen to me. But I ain't so sure. You think, because of the music we got to be too greedy?"

"If that means keeping just about all of myself for me, and as much as I can get from anybody else who's willing to give it, I guess so?"

Another silence.

"Play somethin', Bill."

Bill opened with a phrase that he kept repeating. It reminded Miles of the tune "Some Other Time" in a show from 1944. It wasn't something he would've taken any interest in, except that Bird told him to check it out. Bird was all eyes and ears for just about anything, from eating a flower given to him by a woman who'd come to hear him to quoting Omar Khayyam. Bird believed if you looked and listened long enough, what you pursued would be waiting in your head just when you needed it.

Miles wasn't that taken with "Some Other Time," except when Bill played it. What he loved about Bill's rendition was the detour he took on the fly. That's what he always wanted in any band he led. He never stood for no tired, predictable shit. Miles hummed it into the phone, repeating the initial phrase in his head.

Bill asks a question with the sounds: "Where has the time all gone to?" Answers with, "What I'm doing in this very moment." He steps up his fingerplay, taking a leap to "Haven't done half the things we want to." Both nodding in unison. Bill slows the tinkle from his fingers into "Oh well, we'll catch up some other time." He thinks, "Are we taking this for granted?" Going light in his fingers, he plays "This day was just . . . too many words are still unspoken." Both thinking, "My music speaks well enough for me." Bill delivers, "Just when the fun . . . comes the time for parting." He is all trills on the keys, being ". . . glad for what he has," in the treasure he plays for, and . . . "what is to come," in the craving he might die for, and hovers into a crescendo, ringing in the beauty of church bells … "There's so much more embracing … still to be done, but time is racing."

Back in his Ferrari, Miles listened—to find the places where music is finished before it is done.

*   *   *

In the wee hours of the morning, Frances lay on the bed, still waiting for Miles to come home. She was seized again by the dream she had the night before he was beaten by the police: Fred Astaire and Cyd Charisse's pas de deux in the movie *The Band Wagon*. Charisse was born in Texas, studied ballet since age six. Auditioned for and performed in the Ballets Russes. She was singular in the precision of her movement, stunning with her leg extensions in every performance. *The Band Wagon* was not Frances's favorite movie musical, but the silent dance sequence between Astaire and Charisse was magic.

Astaire and Charisse sitting in a horse-drawn carriage in Central Park, wondering what there is between them. The two leaving the carriage, taking a stroll, lost in their own thoughts, crossing one foot over the other in tandem. Charisse raises her leg into a rond de jambe en l'air, into a chaîné. She looks swept off her feet, but follows with a dizzying series of pirouettes, bringing her face to face, and back to back with Astaire. They never touch. Each movement is a question.

Frances sees herself enter next to Charisse, memorizing her movements step for step. Astaire becomes a blur. Hearing herself, Frances is right there with her foot drags, walks, ball-of-the-foot changes. She executes arabesques, bourrée turns, attitude leg lifts, low plié relevés, promenade lunges. She tells her story until, out of breath, she moves away from Charisse and toward Katherine Dunham …

"You look like you don't belong here, let alone in the same movie with Cyd Charisse," Dunham says.

"I've been away."

"Like I just said."

"I wanted to see if my body remembers what I used to do without thinking."

"And?"

"I'm embarrassed!"

"By what?"

"How much I've forgotten."

"Your body never forgets, even if you do."

"If I forgot, I still remember," Frances says.

"Why didn't Charisse forget how the two go together and you did?"

"She's in a movie."

"But we're not."

"No, we aren't."

"Frances, what do you think is going on here?"

"How I let myself get away from me."

"I'm listening."

"Well, there's a man."

"Stop right there. Why are you bringing a man into this?"

"He's part of my life."

"Why isn't he here?"

"He's supposed to be Astaire."

"What's the name of the sequence in Central Park?"

"'Dancing in the Dark.'"

"You lost sight of Astaire, but not yourself or Charisse."

"I'm more interested in her."

"You mean yourself?"

"Yes."

"So, what about you?"

"I guess I'm here to find out."

"Let's go back to your embarrassment, watching yourself in the mirror. If you agree that your body didn't forget, then what failed you?"

"Myself."

"What were you doing when you danced along with Charisse?"

"Not wanting to make a mistake?"

"So, you were following her?"

"What else could I do?"

"Is that how you learned ballet, watching other people?"

"At first, until I learned how, without watching."

"What was that like?"

"Not having to think about what I'm doing. There's nothing like it!"

"I sensed that when I asked you to join the Company after your audition," Dunham says.

"The only other times I've felt that way was when I rehearsed for my first performance with the Paris Opera Ballet and before the last run through before the opening of West Side Story.*"*

"*Do you think that's what Astaire and Charisse felt about their pas de deux?*"

"*I think so.*"

"*If you feel that way, why would you keep watching them if nothing changed once the movie was made?*"

"*Because I think about how much changed during the rehearsals before the film was finished.*"

"*What about you has changed since your final appearance on stage?*" *Dunham asks.*

"*I was just remembering an evening when the dancers in the Company are waiting in the wings about to go on. I catch a glimpse of that eight-year-old in breathless anticipation, offering a greeting to herself right before offering one to the audience.*"

Frances sees herself back in Central Park, the horse-drawn carriage carrying Charisse and Astaire disappears. She finds herself alone in a dance studio, going through a sequence of moves with all the false steps, starting over, not thinking of anything else except the exhilaration of all the work leading up to an actual performance and hearing Dunham's voice. "What would you say to yourself to express that you're about to rehearse or perform?"

Frances awakens.

"Hello!"

ISBN 978-1-953691-11-8 (hardcover)
ISBN 978-1-953691-14-9 (paperback)

Published by Blank Forms Editions
    in Brooklyn, New York
Designed by Alec Mapes-Frances
Printed by Ofset Yapımevi in
    Istanbul, Turkey

Blank Forms Editions is supported by
the Andy Warhol Foundation for the
Visual Arts, the Robert Rauschenberg
Foundation, and Agnes Gund.